KEEKER
and the Horse Show Show-Off

Book design by Mary Beth Fiorentino.
Typeset in Weiss Medium.
The illustrations in this book were rendered in pen and ink
and then digitally textured.
Manufactured in China.

Library of Congress Cataloging-in-Publication Data
Higginson, Hadley.
Keeker and the horse show show-off / by Hadley Higginson ;
illustrated by Maja Andersen.
p. cm.
Summary: Keeker and her pony Plum enter their very first horse
show, where they are confronted by much more experienced riders.
ISBN-13: 978-0-8118-5135-0 (library edition)
ISBN-10: 0-8118-5135-4 (library edition)
ISBN-13: 978-0-8118-5303-3 (pbk.)
ISBN-10: 0-8118-5303-9 (pbk.)
[1. Horse shows—Fiction. 2. Horsemanship—Fiction.
3. Ponies—Fiction.]
I. Andersen, Maja, ill. II. Title.
PZ7.H53499Kee 2006
[E]—dc22
                                          2005022377

Distributed in Canada by Raincoast Books
9050 Shaughnessy Street, Vancouver, British Columbia V6P 6E5

10 9 8 7 6 5 4 3 2 1

Chronicle Books LLC
85 Second Street, San Francisco, California 94105

www.chroniclekids.com

KEEKER

and the Horse Show Show-Off

by **HADLEY HIGGINSON** Illustrated by **MAJA ANDERSEN**

chronicle books · san francisco

Chapter

1

This is Catherine Corey Keegan Dana, but everyone calls her Keeker. Keeker is nine and one-quarter. She lives in Vermont in a little white house in the country with her mother, her father, five dogs, two cats, a goat, a parakeet and a hamster named Sam. She doesn't have any brothers or sisters but she does have her very own pony, named Plum.

This is Plum. Plum is a Shetland pony who lives in the big field at Keeker's house. Plum has her very own apple tree that she likes to sleep under. She also has a red halter that she's very fond of.

Oh, and she has Keeker.

In the summertime when school is out, Keeker is very busy. She likes going down to the pond to look at tadpoles. She likes going over to her friend Polly's house to put on plays. More than anything, though, she likes riding Plum.

Summertime is busy for Plum, too. She likes rolling in the dirt to scratch all her itches. She likes nibbling apples right off the tree. She likes chasing the goat when he scoots under the fence.

And now that she's trained Keeker, Plum doesn't even mind going riding.

Chapter

2

During the summer, Keeker takes riding
lessons. Twice a week a college student named
Jane Louise Appelgarden comes to Keeker's
house to help with Plum. Jane Louise is very
tidy. She wears riding clothes. She NEVER
looks dirty.

Keeker finds this fascinating because no
matter how clean she tries to stay, she always

ends up with hay in her hair and slobber on her clothes. (Ponies don't drool. But they can be slobbery.)

Jane Louise likes to start every lesson with stretches. "Swing your arms like windmills," she tells Keeker. "Push your heels down, and stretch your neck up tall!"

Sometimes while Keeker is windmilling, Plum will stop walking altogether and put her head down to sneak a snack.

"Silly twirlers," thinks Plum as she munches. "It's SO much more fun to eat grass."

After stretches, Keeker and Plum practice their gaits, which means going at different speeds. Walking and trotting is easy, but it's very hard to make Plum pick up her speed to a canter.

"Give her a kick!" yells Jane Louise. "She's just being stubborn."

Keeker kicks, but Plum just puts her nose in the air and trots faster. *Rat-a-tat-tat.*

One day Keeker and Plum were whizzing in trot circles, when Keeker had a brilliant idea.

"I know what will get Plum going," she said. "Let's try jumping!"

Jane Louise agreed that this was just the thing to do. She took two hay bales out of the barn and placed them end to end, making a fuzzy-looking horse jump.

"Okay, Keeker," said Jane Louise. "Trot once around the jump; then turn toward it, and give her a big kick! Remember to stand up in your

stirrups a little and release the reins like
I showed you."

Keeker and Plum trotted once around then
headed toward the jump.

"Are those for eating?" Plum wondered as
they trotted toward the bales. "Surely I'm not
supposed to go OVER them?"

"Yikes!" thought Keeker. She closed her
eyes and crossed her fingers and gave Plum a
BIG kick. Plum was startled; she snorted and
bucked and charged toward the bales. Keeker
and Plum flew over them.

Chapter

3

After that, Keeker and Plum jumped at every single lesson. Jane Louise used all kinds of things to build jumps: tires, fence rails, barrels, hay bales—she even used flowerpots.

Sometimes in the evening, Plum jumped in and out of her stall just for fun. Sometimes in the morning, Keeker jumped up and down the stairs, even though it drove her mom nuts.

One day right after Keeker's riding lesson, something very interesting came in the mail.

It was a green-and-white flyer announcing the 4-H horse show.

Keeker was so excited she had to hop around for a minute. If she went to a horse show, she would get to wear fancy riding clothes. She might even win a blue ribbon to hang on her wall.

Plum thought it was a dumb idea. "Horse shows are for show-offs," she sniffed.

The horse show was in three weeks, so there was a lot to do. First, Keeker and her mother went over to Keeker's cousin's house to borrow riding pants and a riding coat.

Then Jane Louise showed Keeker how to polish her boots and clean her saddle so the leather looked shiny.

"I'm going to look so fancy!" thought Keeker. She was thrilled.

"What a lot of fuss," grumped Plum. "I'd rather stay home and eat apples."

In between polishings, Keeker practiced
her acceptance speech, for when she would be
awarded the blue ribbon.

"I'd like to thank my parents and, especially,
my riding teacher, Jane Louise. . . ."

Plum prepared for the horse show by taking a few extra dirt baths. But secretly, when no one was looking, she practiced flaring her nostrils so that she looked wild, the way a real show jumper would.

And sometimes she peeked at her reflection to see if she looked like a champion.

Chapter
4

The night before the horse show, Keeker could barely sleep. She tossed and turned and had crazy dreams.

In one dream, she was riding Plum while wearing a long pink dress, and every time they went over a jump, the dress fanned out behind them like a peacock's tail. (Plum was very light and floaty, almost as though she was flying.)

In another dream, Plum was walking around on her hind legs, talking just like Jane Louise. She even had Jane Louise's sunglasses on!

Over in the barn, Plum wasn't getting much sleep either. But it wasn't because she was nervous; it was because there was a barn owl up in the rafters, hooting away.

"Hoo-hoo-HOO!" called the barn owl, peering down into Plum's stall. "HOO!"

"Shush!" Plum snorted. She tucked her head under her hay pile, but it didn't do much good.

The next morning Keeker felt GREAT even though she'd gotten barely any sleep. She took a shower and got dressed and ate breakfast as fast as she could. She was ready!

Plum woke up groggy and grumpy, with hay in her hair. One of her legs was asleep, and she had a knot in her tail.

When Plum realized she had to get on the horse trailer, she was doubly grumpy.

"I'm not getting back on that old rattly clank," Plum huffed.

It took Keeker, her mother, her father, two of the dogs and a LOT of carrots to make Plum get on the trailer. But finally she was on.

"Carrots make everything better," thought
Plum as she crunched.

And they were on their way.

Chapter 5

When they got to the fairgrounds, Keeker's mom took Keeker and Plum to the barns where Plum would be stabled during the show.

Keeker and Plum had stall number 37. Right next door to them, in stall number 36, was a shiny dapple gray pony.

Sitting outside the stall on a hay bale was a girl dressed in fancy clothes.

36

37

"Hi," said the girl. "My name's Tifni with an *i*. What's your name?"

"Ummm, Keeker," said Keeker. "Keeker with two *e*'s."

"This is my pony," said Tifni. "She's SO new; I just got her last month. Her name is Lulu's Li'l Windsong."

Windsong popped her head over the top of the stall door and sniffed delicately. She was very pretty, Keeker had to admit.

"I've already won SO many ribbons this year, with my other pony," said Tifni. "Wanna see?"

She opened the top of her tack trunk and pulled out three ribbons and one shiny silver trophy.

Keeker began to feel a little anxious. She had never won a single ribbon. In fact, all she had in her tack trunk was a sandwich her dad had made her (PB&J on white bread, no crust) and an apple for Plum.

"Well, it's time to start getting ready, so I guess I'll see you in the warm-up ring," said Tifni. "Byyyyyyeee!"

Just then Jane Louise and Keeker's mom showed up to help Keeker with Plum. They were in a very good mood; they laughed and chatted and seemed very excited.

Keeker was suddenly not in a good mood. She kept sneaking peeks over to Tifni's stall, and everything Tifni was putting on her pony seemed much fancier and shinier than what they were putting on Plum.

Plum was not in a good mood either. Her leg was still asleep, and her saddle felt pinchy. Plus, she was hungry.

In all the excitement of the morning, no one had remembered to feed her.

"Harrumph," groused Plum. Her stomach grumbled and rumbled, and no one—not Keeker, not Keeker's mom, not even Jane Louise—seemed to notice.

Chapter

6

When Plum was all tacked up, Jane Louise gave Keeker a leg up (for luck), and they all walked over to the warm-up ring.

There were a zillion ponies there—Keeker had never seen so many ponies and kids all in one place in her life!

But even in the crowd, it was easy to spot Tifni. She had blue velvet ribbons on the

ends of her braids and blue yarn braided into
Windsong's mane.

Keeker began to feel very sad. She didn't
have any ribbons in her hair, and she wasn't
wearing any new stuff.

Plum's mane wasn't even braided—it was just
sticking out like it normally did.

"Everyone looks better than me," Keeker
thought miserably.

"These ponies look ridiculous," thought Plum.
"Everyone here could use a good roll in the dirt."

Suddenly, the announcer called, "Number thirty-six, you're on deck!" That meant Tifni and Windsong were up next. They rode into the starting gate, and *DING!* the starting bell clanged.

Off they went. Tifni and her pony jumped the first jump perfectly. Then the second, then the third, then the fourth, then the fifth.

The sixth jump was right in front of the judge's stand. Tifni turned sideways in her saddle to give the judges a BIG smile.

But, turning sideways in your saddle isn't
always such a good idea. Windsong turned
sideways, too, and missed the last jump entirely.

"Ohhhhhhhhh," the crowd groaned. Tifni's
mother gasped and clutched her purse.
She looked like she might faint. Tifni burst
into tears.

"BAD pony!" she said as she rode out of the ring, even though it really wasn't Windsong's fault.

That made Windsong VERY mad. So mad, in fact, that she nipped Plum on the nose as they rode by.

Chapter

7

Plum had had enough. It was one thing to miss your breakfast and have your leg fall asleep; it was quite another to get bitten by a snotty pony you didn't even know.

"Time to teach those two a lesson," she thought.

Keeker and Plum rode into the starting gate. Plum snorted and pawed and swished her tail—

she was ready! Keeker sat in a slumpy way. She felt like crying. She wished she were at home, riding in the field. She couldn't even remember why she had wanted to come to the horse show in the first place.

The starting bell clanged, and Keeker and Plum were off. Plum flew over the first jump, then the second, then the third. Keeker stopped slumping. She sat up and pushed her heels down and stretched her neck up tall, just like Jane Louise had said.

They jumped the fourth jump and the fifth, then SAILED over the last jump like they were in the Olympics. Even the judges cheered!

Had they won? It seemed too good to be true. The loudspeaker crackled with static, and the announcer's voice came on loud and clear: "Our winner is . . . number thirty-seven!"

That was Keeker's number—they HAD
won! Keeker was so surprised she forgot all
about her acceptance speech.

Plum wasn't surprised at all. She stood
perfectly still and puffed her chest out proudly
as the judge pinned the blue ribbon onto
her bridle.

That night Keeker and her parents and Jane
Louise all went out for burgers, to celebrate.
Keeker saved her pickles for Plum.

Plum LOVED pickles. Keeker brought them
down to the barn, and Plum nibbled them
gently out of her hand.

After that, everyone was full and sleepy. Keeker went back to the house and got under her delicious cool covers and drifted off immediately. Plum pushed her hay into a pile and fell asleep on top of it.

Even the barn owl couldn't stay awake.

The stars in the sky glittered like silver trophies. The whole night long they winked and blinked, all the way till morning.